DATE DUE

10004   MAY 0 1 2001

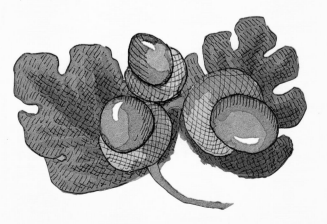

For Felix
H.O.

For Nan
A.R.

WHAT'S NAUGHTY?
by Hiawyn Oram and Adrian Reynolds
British Library Cataloguing in Publication Data
A catalogue record of this book is available from the British Library.
ISBN 0 340 75446 X (HB)
ISBN 0 340 75447 8 (PB)

Text copyright © Hiawyn Oram 2000
Illustrations copyright © Adrian Reynolds 2000

The right of Hiawyn Oram to be identified as the author
and Adrian Reynolds as the illustrator of this Work
has been asserted by them in accordance with
the Copyright, Designs and Patents Act 1988.

First edition published 2000
10 9 8 7 6 5 4 3 2

Published by Hodder Children's Books,
a division of Hodder Headline Limited,
338 Euston Road, London NW1 3BH

Printed in Hong Kong

What's Naughty?

Written by Hiawyn Oram

Illustrated by Adrian Reynolds

*Hodder
Children's
Books*

A division of Hodder Headline Limited

William was over at Alex's house.
"Now you two go outside and play
and don't be naughty," said Alex's mother.
"OK!" said Alex and Will.

They ran outside and found a rusty old bath
full of rusty old water beside the back hedge.
"Let's jump in and out of it," said Alex.

"What, till our shoes are soaked,
like this?" said Will.
"And we are soaked, like this," said Alex.

They spotted a snail crawling up the wall,
leaving a long silver trail.
"Let's make it start all over again," said Alex.

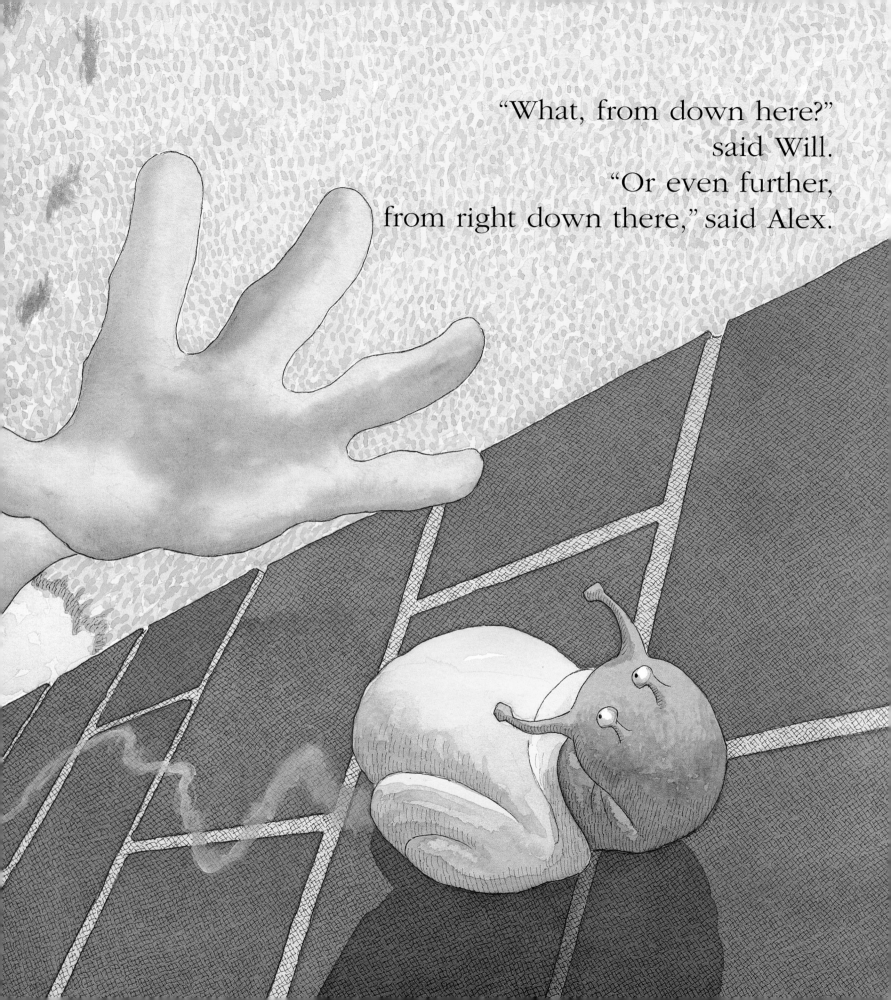

"What, from down here?"
said Will.
"Or even further,
from right down there," said Alex.

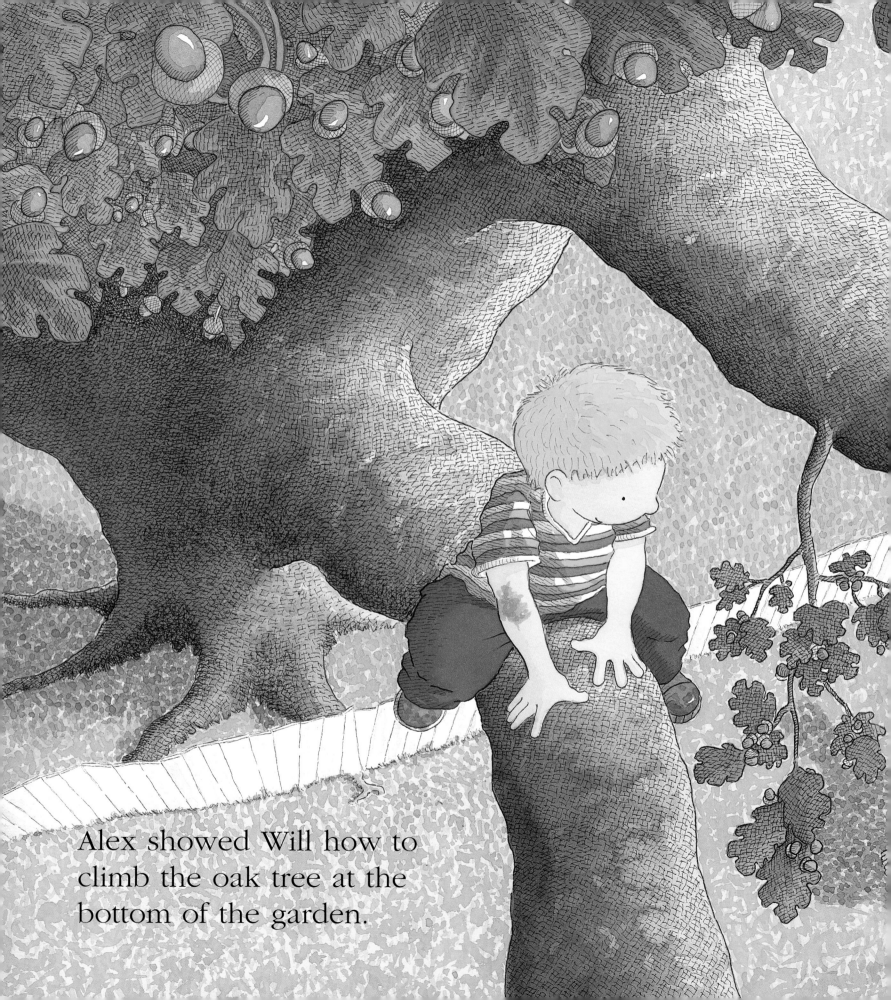

Alex showed Will how to climb the oak tree at the bottom of the garden.

"Oh, look," said Alex. "There's our neighbour,
fast asleep in his chair."
"Let's wake him up," said Will.
"What, like this?" said Alex, dropping an acorn.
"Yeah, and like this," said Will, shaking a
whole branch of acorns down on him.

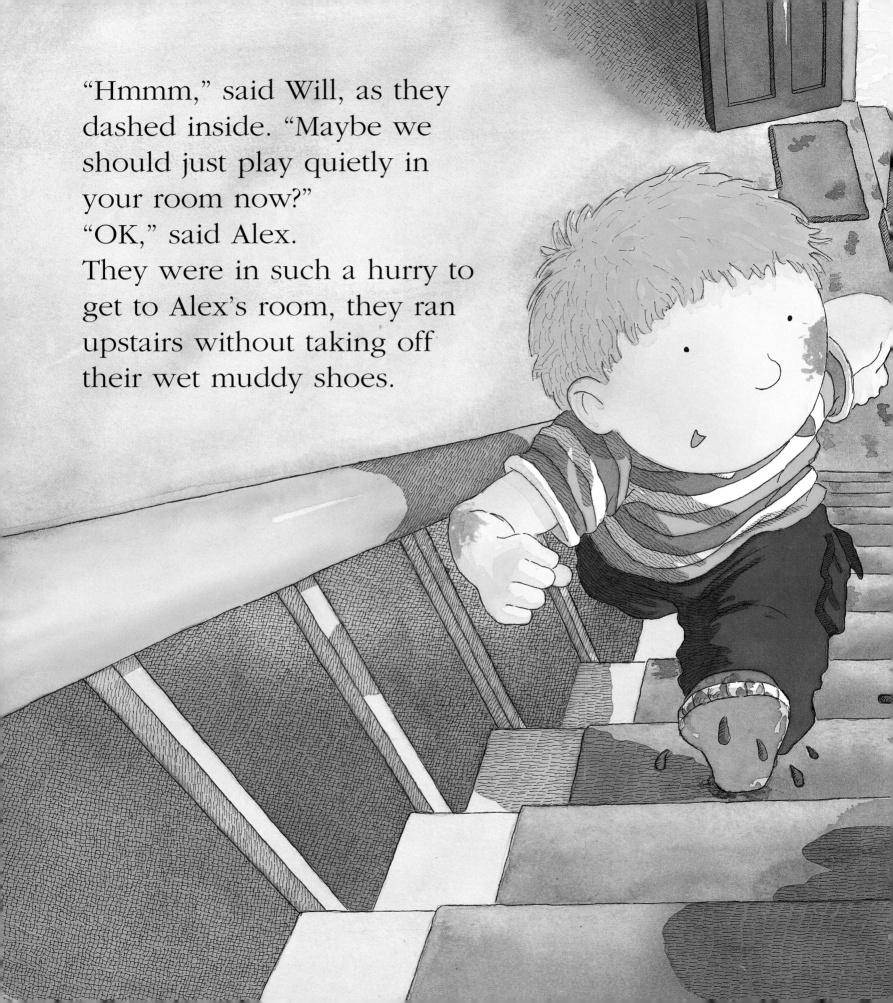

"Hmmm," said Will, as they dashed inside. "Maybe we should just play quietly in your room now?"

"OK," said Alex.

They were in such a hurry to get to Alex's room, they ran upstairs without taking off their wet muddy shoes.

"Hey, where's that helicopter of yours?"
said Will. "The blue one with the bent propeller?"
"It's in here somewhere," said Alex.
They tipped out every toy in Alex's room but
they couldn't find the helicopter.
"Never mind," said Alex. "Let's play that
sliding game of ours, down the stairs."
"OK," said Will.

Alex got the duvet from his bed
and the duvet from his sister's bed.
"I'll have the big one," he said.
"OK, I'll have the second biggest," said Will.
They played the duvet-sliding game
until they heard a splitting noise.
"Whoops," said Will.
"Don't worry," said Alex.
"I know where the glue is."

The glue was in the tidy-drawer
in Alex's mother's dressing table.
While Alex glued the duvet cover,
Will had a look at all her pots
and jars and bottles.
"You could make a good
potion with these,"
he said.

"What, to ward off wicked wizards?" said Alex.
"And warty toads," said Will.
"And alien vampires," said Alex.
"And graveyard ghouly things," said Will.
So, while the duvet dried, Alex got a mixing bowl and two spoons . . .

. . . and they began mixing a Warding-Off Potion
to ward off every wicked, warty, alien, ghouly thing
in the world.
They were just adding some extra glittery bits when
they heard Alex's mother calling them for tea.
"I'm so hungry I could eat a truckload," said Will.
"I'm so hungry I could eat two truckloads,"
said Alex.
So they forgot about warding
off things and ran
downstairs for tea.

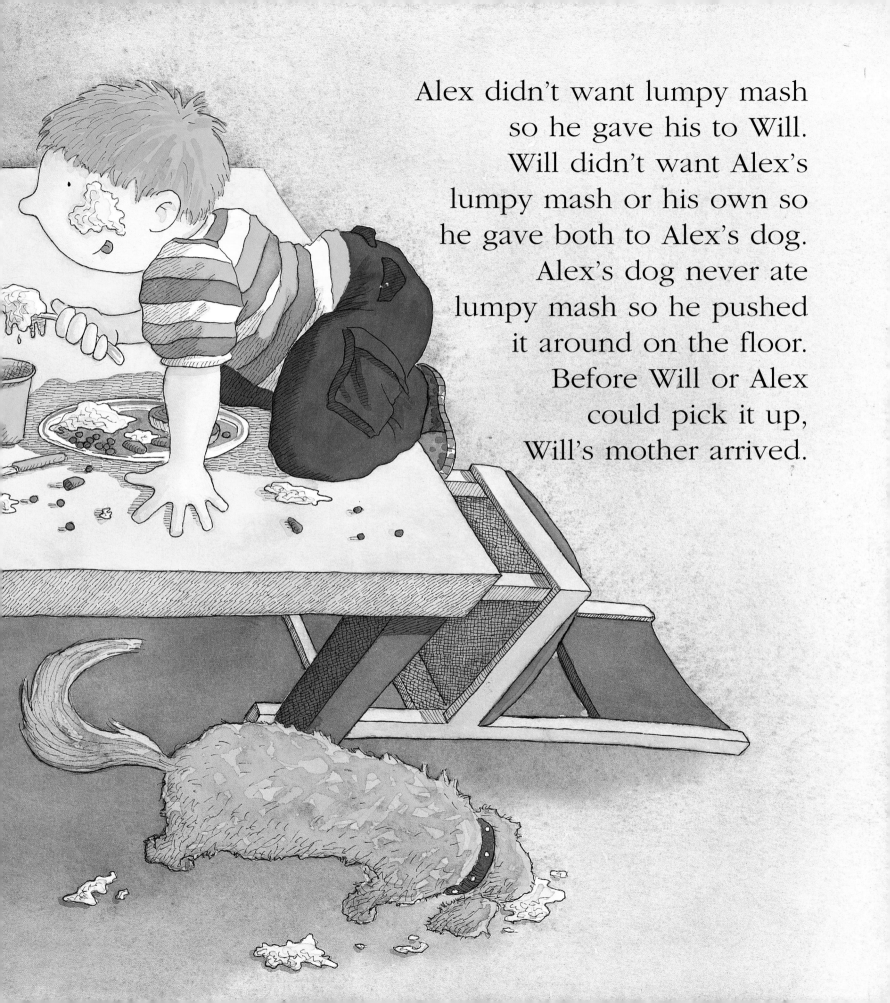

Alex didn't want lumpy mash
so he gave his to Will.
Will didn't want Alex's
lumpy mash or his own so
he gave both to Alex's dog.
Alex's dog never ate
lumpy mash so he pushed
it around on the floor.
Before Will or Alex
could pick it up,
Will's mother arrived.

"Cooey!" she called. "Have they been good boys?"
"Good as gold," said Alex's mother,
folding her arms in her special
let's-have-a-good-long-chat way.
"Hey," whispered Alex, "shall we go outside
and see how our snail's getting on?"

"Yeah," whispered Will, "'cos what I'd like to know
is where all its silvery slime comes from
in the first place?"
"And what I'd like to know," whispered Alex,
"is if we've been good . . .

. . . what's naughty?"

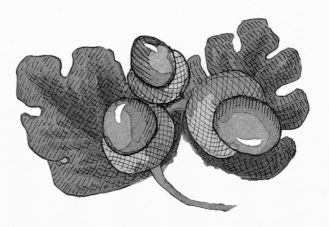